D1389833

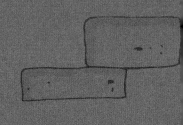

PEUK 2327

Published by Ladybird Books Ltd
A Penguin Company
Penguin Books Ltd, 80 Strand, London, WC2R ORL, England
Penguin Books Australia Ltd, Camberwell, Victoria, Australia
Penguin Group (NZ), cnr Airborne and Rosedale Roads,
Albany, Auckland 1310, New Zealand
All rights reserved

ISBN-13: 978-1-84422-640-5
ISBN-10: 1-8442-2640-9

4 6 8 10 9 7 5

Ladybird and the device of a ladybird are trademarks
of Ladybird Books Ltd

Printed in Italy

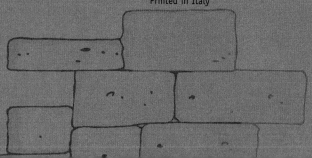

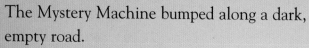

The Mystery Machine bumped along a dark, empty road.

"Like, we're in the middle of nowhere!" said Shaggy. "I hope we have enough gas!"

All at once, the van stopped.

"Roh-oh!" said Scooby.

"Engine trouble. We have to call a tow truck,"
said Fred. Velma and Daphne looked around.
Where could they find a telephone?
"Rook!" Scooby cried, pointing. "A right!"
"Maybe it's a house with a phone," said Velma.
"And a fridge," Shaggy added.

The gang walked toward the light.
It was growing brighter and brighter.
They were getting closer.
Suddenly, Velma said, "Jinkies!
It's not a house. It's a castle!"
The castle looked really spooky.
Scooby dug in his paws. He didn't
want to move.

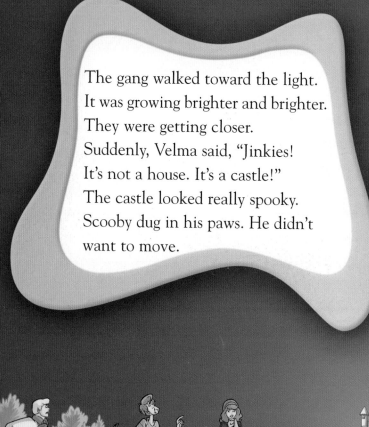

"Come on, old buddy," Shaggy said. "Think fridge! Think snacks!"
In a flash, Scooby swam across the moat and banged on the drawbridge with his tail.

The drawbridge dropped. There were three
suits of armour standing at the door.
"Cool statues," said Shaggy.
Clank, clank. The helmets snapped open.
They weren't suits of armour. They were
knights. Shiny spooky knights!

"Come on," said Fred. "We have to find a phone."

Scooby shook his head. "Ro way."

"For a Scooby Snack?" Velma asked.

Shaggy, Fred and Scooby raced inside.

In the castle's great hall, a
chandelier swung back and
forth. Creak, creak.
"That's funny," said Daphne.
"There's no breeze. What is
making it move?"

"Ghosts!" whispered Scooby as a strange man rushed into the room.

As the man opened his mouth to speak, Scooby saw his sharp, pointy teeth.

"Rangs!" said Scooby.

"He's a vampire!" Shaggy cried, running away.

"Like, since we're running… " Shaggy said,
"let's run to the kitchen."
"Reah!" said Scooby.
In the kitchen, they saw a woman.
She stirred a big pot that bubbled over a fire.

"A witch!" cried Shaggy.

"You two are perfect!" said the witch. "Just what I need."

"No way," said Shaggy. "We're not part of your spooky recipe!"

Shaggy and Scooby
quickly raced away.
"Stop!" cried the witch.
"Stop!" cried the
vampire as they
chased Shaggy and
Scooby.

Shaggy and Scooby backed into a corner.

Suddenly, a mummy leapt up.

"Time is up!" he shouted.

"Our time is up, Scoob," Shaggy wailed.

"We've got to get out of here!"

They raced up the stairs.
"Stop!" cried the mummy.
"Stop!" cried the witch.
"Stop!" cried the vampire.
"Let's find Velma, Fred and
Daphne. Then we'll get outta
here," said Shaggy.

Finally, Shaggy flung open a door. Down below, they saw monsters and zombies and ghosts…

…and Velma, Daphne and Fred!
A knight was standing over them. He held his
sword tight.

"What should we do?"
Shaggy asked Scooby.
Just then the vampire,
witch and mummy
leaped beside them.

"Rump!" said Scooby.

"Jump?" Shaggy yelled.

Shaggy grabbed the chandelier.

Scooby grabbed Shaggy.

They swung across the room.

Shaggy and Scooby dropped to the floor...
right on top of the knight!
"My sword!" the knight cried.
"Grab it, Fred!" Shaggy shouted.
Fred scooped it up. But then he gave it back
to the knight!

Scooby hid his eyes. He was afraid to look.

"Relax," Velma said. "The knight is going to cut the cake."

Velma stepped out of the way. Now Shaggy could see a party cake!

"It's a costume party!" Velma said.

"But," said Shaggy, "what about the ghostly chandelier?"

"I was pulling a string," said the vampire,
"to move the chandelier into place."
"And the witch's potion?" Shaggy asked.
"Punch!" said the witch. "I wanted you to
try it."

"And the mummy's warning, 'Time is up?'"
The mummy smiled, "My nap time was over!"
"But you chased us!" said Shaggy.
"To invite you to the party," said the vampire.
"Uh, we knew it all along, right, Scooby?"
said Shaggy. "We were just acting."

Scooby looked around at all the smiling faces.
He stood up and bowed. "Scooby-Dooby-Doo!"
"Would you like to use the phone now?" asked
the knight.
"Uh, no rush," said Shaggy. "How about a nice
big piece of that cake?"